BASKETBALL
AND OTHER
BALL SPORTS

by Clive Gifford

amicus

Published by Amicus
P.O. Box 1329
Mankato, MN 56002

Printed in the United States of America, at Corporate Graphics in North Mankato, Minnesota.

Library of Congress Cataloging-in-Publication Data
Gifford, Clive.
  Basketball and other ball sports / by Clive Gifford.
     p. cm. -- (Olympic sports)
  Summary: "An introduction to a variety of ball sports of the summer Olympics, including field hockey, volleyball, tennis, basketball, and more. Also explains rules, records, and famous Olympic athletes in each sport." --Provided by publisher.
  Includes index.
  ISBN 978-1-60753-188-3 (hardcover, library binding)
  1. Ball games--Juvenile literature. 2. Olympics--Juvenile literature. I. Title.
  GV861.G54 2012
  796.35--dc22

                                                                    2010035131

Created by Appleseed Editions, Ltd.
Designed by Helen James
Edited by Mary-Jane Wilkins
Picture research by Su Alexander

Picture credits
Page 4 Sports Illustrated/Getty Images; 5t Sunxuejun/Shutterstock, b AFP/Getty Images; 6 AFP/Getty Images; 7 Sports Illustrated/Getty Images; 8 Bongarts/Getty Images for DFB; 9 The FA via Getty Images; 10 & 11 Getty Images; 12 & 13 NBAE/Getty Images; 14 Bloomberg via Getty Images; 15 & 16 AFP/Getty Images; 17 Olga Besnard/Shutterstock; 18 Getty Images; 19,20,21,22,23 & 24 AFP/Getty Images; 25 Muzsy/Shutterstock; 26 Getty Images; 27 AFP/Getty Images; 28 Lev Radin/Shutterstock; 29t Getty Images, b Brandon Parry/Shutterstock
Front cover: Getty Images

DAD0051
3-2011

9 8 7 6 5 4 3 2 1

Contents

Going for Gold

The Olympics is the greatest sports show on Earth. More than 10,000 athletes (or Olympians) flock to one country, where they live in an Olympic village and compete against each other during 17 days of unforgettable action. The top performers win an Olympic gold, silver, or bronze medal for finishing in the top three of their event.

The women's beach volleyball medal winners wave to the crowd at the 2008 Olympics. In the center are gold medalists Kerri Walsh and Misty May-Treanor from the United States.

MODERN GAMES

The modern Olympic Games began in 1896 in Athens. They revived the sports contests held by the ancient Greeks at Olympia from 776 BC.

Today, the Olympics are held during the summer every four years. The host city and nation welcome thousands of spectators, while hundreds of millions more watch on television.

BALL SPORTS BOOM

The 1896 Olympics included just one ball sport—men's tennis. The winner, John Pius Boland, was in Greece on vacation and only decided to take part in the tennis competition at the last minute. Today, more than a thousand athletes take part in a range of ball sports, both individually and on teams, in every Olympics.

The Beijing National Stadium was used for the 2008 Olympics opening ceremony, athletic events, and soccer finals.

IN OR OUT?

Some ball sports that were once part of the Olympics are no longer played at the games. They include cricket, lacrosse, croquet, and polo on horseback. Baseball and softball were played until 2008, but they will not be part of the 2012 or 2016 games. Two ball sports will rejoin the Olympics in 2016—golf for top **professionals** and a form of rugby union called rugby sevens; this is a seven-a-side version of the sport. The teams play on the full-sized rugby pitch, which is usually used by 15-player teams.

Argentina's Lionel Messi (right) runs with the ball during the final of the men's soccer competition against Nigeria at the 2008 games.

FEATS AND RECORDS

Did you know that the U.S. is the reigning Olympic rugby union champion? They won the competition in 1924, the last time it was held. France won silver, and Romania won bronze.

Soccer

The world's most popular team sport has been played at the Olympics since 1900 by men and since 1996 by women. At the 2008 Olympics, a record 2,137,462 spectators watched the two tournaments.

Italy's Giuseppe Rossi takes a penalty kick against Belgium in the quarter finals of the 2008 Olympics. Rossi scored two penalty shots in this game, but his team lost 3–2.

AIM OF THE GAME

A soccer game lasts 90 minutes, with a 15-minute break at halftime. Teams play by moving the ball around the field using any part of their bodies except their arms and hands. The goalkeepers are allowed to use their hands, but only inside the penalty area—the box surrounding their goal. The offensive team scores by shooting or heading the ball into the opponents' goal. The defending team tries to stop goals from being scored against it and to gain control of the ball.

A coach or manager decides the team's **formation**. This is the way the team lines up in rows of **defenders**, **midfielders**, and **forwards**.

Christie Rampone (right) about to tackle Brazil's Renata Costa during the 2008 Olympic final. Rampone was captain of the U.S. team, which won 1–0 and the gold medal.

goal

penalty area

penalty spot

center circle

Soccer fields vary in length between 295 and 395 feet (90–120 m). Fields are split in half, and each end has a 132.2 ft. (40.3 m) wide penalty area around the goal.

eight teams entering the **knockout** rounds (quarter finals, semi-finals, and the final). In the knockout stages, a tied game goes into overtime, and if the scores are still tied, there is a **penalty** shoot-out. Each team takes five penalties, and if neither team pulls ahead, there is a sudden death shoot-out. Only one Olympic final has been decided this way, when Cameroon beat Spain 5–3 on penalties in 2000.

Tactics can change during a game, and the coach can swap up to three players with **substitutes** to keep the players strong.

IT'S A KNOCKOUT

Sixteen teams take part in the men's Olympics soccer tournament and twelve in the women's. They are placed in groups of four with the top

Olympic OoPs

A combined Great Britain team competed in the Olympics until 1972. In 1952 they suffered an embarrassing defeat against Luxembourg 5–3. Their worst ever Olympic defeat was in the 1956 games when they lost 6–1 to Bulgaria.

German forward Birgit Prinz (center) powers forward between two Danish defenders. Prinz holds the record for the most goals scored in a single Olympic game (four against China in 2004). She shares this record with Brazil's Cristiane.

FEATS AND RECORDS

The U.S. women's team has lost just two of 24 games at four Olympics. They won gold medals in 1996, 2004, and 2008, and silver in 2000.

EARLY CHAMPIONS

During the 1920s, a strong team from Uruguay won the gold in the 1924 and 1928 Olympics, and then the first **World Cup** in 1930. After World War II, eastern European nations won every tournament from 1952 to 1988, except in 1984, when France won.

PROS ALLOWED

Only **amateur** soccer players were allowed to compete in the games until 1984. Today, all 18 players on a team can be professional, but at least 15 must be under 23 years old. Ronaldinho, for example, was 28 years old when he played

Superstar

In 2000, Cameroon goalkeeper Idris Kameni became the youngest ever soccer gold medalist. He was just 16 years old. Eight years earlier, Sammy Kuffour from Ghana won a bronze medal at the age of 15.

for Brazil at the 2008 Olympics and won a bronze medal. There are no age restrictions in the women's tournament, so top female stars such as Brazil's Marta and U.S. legend Mia Hamm can play.

The 2012 Olympic soccer final will be played at the new Wembley Stadium in the UK. Other games will be played at Manchester United's Old Trafford stadium, the Millennium Stadium in Cardiff, Hampden Park, Glasgow, and St James's Park, Newcastle.

SHOCKING RESULTS

Soccer games can be low-scoring and can have unexpected results. At the 2004 Olympics, Iraq knocked out a Portuguese team that included Cristiano Ronaldo, and **underdogs** Paraguay beat Italy 1–0, reaching the final of the men's tournament.

Basketball

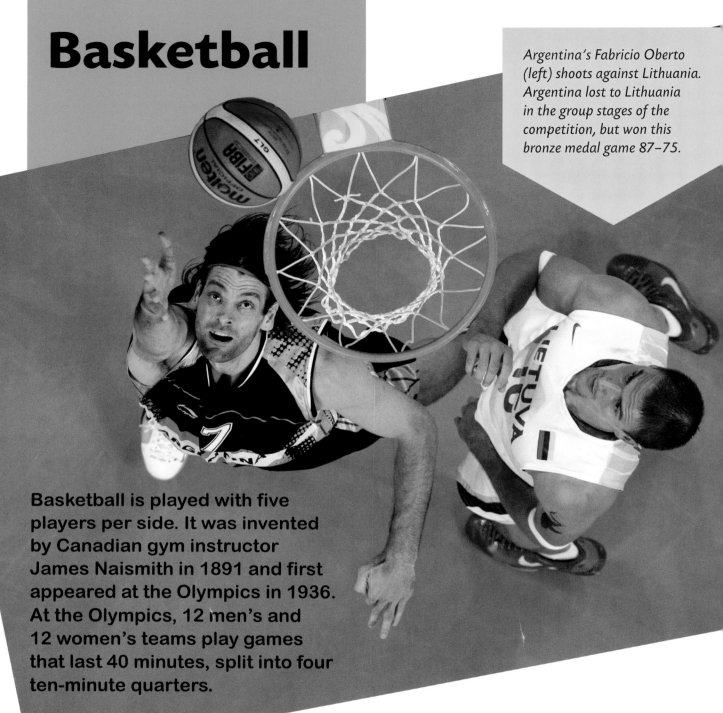

Basketball is played with five players per side. It was invented by Canadian gym instructor James Naismith in 1891 and first appeared at the Olympics in 1936. At the Olympics, 12 men's and 12 women's teams play games that last 40 minutes, split into four ten-minute quarters.

COURT SPORT

At the Olympics, basketball games are played on a 92 ft. (28 m) long court, split in half, with a high hoop at each end. Players score baskets by shooting the ball through the hoop from above. Shots made from within a D-shaped arc, called the three point line, at each end of the court score two points. Shots from outside the arc score three points.

Players move the basketball around the court by **passing** it to teammates, or **dribble** by bouncing the ball with one hand as they move. Once they start dribbling, players cannot stop, hold the ball, and start to dribble again. If they do, the ball goes to their opponents. Players use a range of chest, bounce, and overhead passes over different distances. They also make fake moves or passes to trick opponents.

COUNTING DOWN

Basketball games are quick, sharp, and ferocious. Teams have just 24 seconds from when they receive the ball to make a shot, otherwise the ball goes to the other team. The time is displayed on a clock, and as the seconds count down, the tension rises. The defending team tries to **intercept** weak passes to gain the ball and each defender may **mark** an area or an opponent to stop them from getting the ball.

FEATS AND RECORDS
The women's U.S. and Australian teams have competed in the final of the last three Olympics, with the Australians having to settle for silver every time.

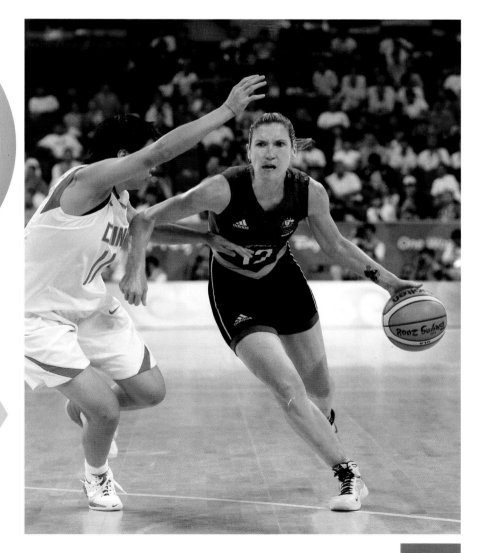

Lauren Jackson of Australia dribbles the ball as she drives forward past a Chinese defender. Australia won this 2008 semi-final match, but lost 92–65 in the final.

In the 2008 Olympic final, Spain's Pau Gasol has both hands on the ball as he is guarded by the U.S.'s Jason Kidd. Both Gasol, who stands 7 ft. (2.13 m) tall, and Kidd play in the NBA.

FEATS AND RECORDS

Lithuania is one of the smallest countries ever to reach the Olympic basketball tournament —fewer than 3.5 million people live there. Their Olympic teams have won three bronze medals and come in fourth twice in the last five Olympics.

REBOUNDS

When a shot misses and the ball bounces off the hoop or the backboard behind, both teams compete for the ball. This is called rebounding. A team that wins the most rebounds usually wins the game. At the 2008 Olympics, Iran's Hamed Haddadi grabbed an average of more than 11 rebounds every game.

GIANTS OF THE GAME

Top basketball players are tall, often over 6'5" (1.95 m) in height. The tallest woman to win an Olympic gold medal in any sport was Soviet basketball player Iuliana Semenova. She stood 7'2" (2.18 m) tall and won gold in both 1976 and 1980. In the men's game, China's Yao Ming is one of the tallest players ever—a towering 7'6" (2.29 m) tall.

BASKETBALL LEAGUES

Away from the Olympics, the world's leading professional league is the National Basketball Association (NBA) in North America. Many foreign stars play for NBA teams, including Spain's Pau Gasol, Argentina's Manu Ginobili, and Britain's Luol Deng. A similar league for female players, the WNBA, began in 1997. Lauren Jackson, captain of the Australian team and an Olympic silver medalist, plays in the WNBA.

DREAM TEAMS

Professional basketball players were first allowed to compete in the 1992 Olympics, in Barcelona, Spain. The U.S. "dream team" included top NBA stars such as Michael Jordan, Magic Johnson, and Larry Bird. They won the tournament easily. Since then, U.S. Olympic teams have included talented players such as Shaquille O'Neal, Kevin Garnett, and Kobe Bryant.

They have won gold medals at every Olympic games, except 2004. There, Lithuania, Puerto Rico, and Argentina all defeated the U.S. team, and Argentina took the gold medal.

Basketball legends Michael Jordan (left) and Magic Johnson celebrate during the 1992 Barcelona Olympics. The U.S. Dream Team scored more than 100 points in every one of their eight games.

Tennis

Tennis players competed at the Olympics from 1896 to 1924. After a gap of 64 years, tennis was played again at the 1988 Olympics in Seoul, South Korea. Miloslav Mecir and Steffi Graf won gold medals in the singles.

Swiss tennis player Roger Federer (right) with partner Stanislas Wawrinka face Americans Bob and Mike Bryan in their 2008 Olympic semi-final match. Federer and Wawrinka won the match 7–6, 6–4.

SERVE AND RETURN

Tennis players compete on a rectangular court that is 78 ft. (23.8 m) long and divided in two by a net. They hit the ball over the net with stringed rackets. Each point starts with one player hitting a **serve**, a powerful overhead shot from behind the back line of the court into their opponent's service court. Some powerful servers, such as Andy Roddick from the U.S., can strike the ball at speeds of over 143 miles per hour (230 km/h)!

RALLIES

Once the ball is in play, a **rally** begins. Each player strikes the ball, trying to hit a winning shot that the opponent cannot reach. Top players need to be fit and **agile** so they can change direction quickly and chase down the ball. Some rallies are over in a short, sharp series of two or three shots. Others last 15 or more shots. Matches in the Olympics can last three hours or longer, so players also need great **stamina**.

Superstar

Roger Federer is considered to be one of the best male tennis players of all time. He has won 16 **grand slam** singles titles, but never the Olympic singles competition. He met his wife, tennis player Mirka Vavrinec, at the 2000 Olympics and in 2008 won the doubles with fellow Swiss tennis player Stanislas Wawrinka.

SINGLES AND DOUBLES

A total of 64 men and 64 women take part in Olympic singles tournaments. These are the top players in the world rankings. A handful of players, such as those returning after an injury, are given a **wild card** that allows them to compete. Thirty-two pairs of men and women compete the doubles. In 2012, there will be a mixed doubles competition, too.

doubles sideline

singles sideline

baseline

service line

net

center service line

A tennis court has two sets of sidelines. The wider lines are used in doubles matches, and the narrower ones are used in singles matches.

FEATS AND RECORDS

Only one tennis player has won both the singles and doubles at the same Olympic Games since 1988—Chile's Nicolás Massú in 2004.

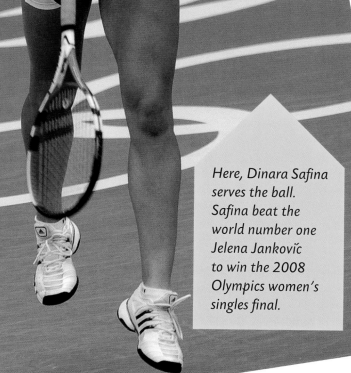

Here, Dinara Safina serves the ball. Safina beat the world number one Jelena Jankovič to win the 2008 Olympics women's singles final.

Elena Dementieva shows her delight as she wins an Olympic gold medal in 2008. She beat Dinara Safina in the final: 3–6, 7–5, 6–3. Dementieva also won a silver medal at the 2000 Olympics.

FEATS AND RECORDS

Elena Dementieva won the women's singles at the 2008 games, and fellow Russians Dinara Safina and Vera Zvonareva took silver and bronze. This was the first time one country won all three singles medals since 1908.

SCORING SYSTEM

Tennis has an unusual scoring system. A match is broken down into sets of games. At the Olympics, a player has to win two sets to beat an opponent. Players who reach the finals of the men's singles and doubles have to win three sets to take the match. To win a set, players have to win six games and be at least two games ahead of their opponent, so 6–4 and 7–5 are set-winning scores. If the players win six games each, they play a **tiebreaker** to decide who takes the set. When they reach 6–6 in the fifth set of a final or the third set of other matches, players have to continue until one wins two more games than their opponent.

ON TOUR

Besides the Olympics, the top tennis players take part in men's (ATP) and women's (WTA) professional tours and play tournaments almost every week from January to November. Dotted throughout the year are four tournaments rated higher than the rest—the Australian Open, the French Open, Wimbledon, and the U.S. Open. These four are grand-slam tournaments, and they are the tournaments that tennis players most want to win.

GREAT IMPORTANCE

Only 11 of the world's top 20 men competed at the 1988 Olympics, and only three of the top ten men competed in 1996. Today, players who compete at an Olympics win points that count toward their position on the professional tour. The 2008 singles competitions included 17 of the top 20 men, and 18 of the top 20 women.

FEATS AND RECORDS

Lleyton Hewitt and Chris Guccione played 57 games to beat Agustin Calleri and Juan Monaco at the 2008 Olympics men's doubles (4–6, 7–6, 18–16). This was the highest number of games ever played in a three-set match at an Olympics.

BRONZE PLAY-OFF

In 1988 and 1992, the two losers at the semi-final stage both received a bronze medal. Since then, the two have to play a further match to decide who wins the bronze. In 2000, Frenchman Arnaud Di Pasquale beat Roger Federer to win the bronze.

Rafael Nadal of Spain hits a powerful forehand. In 2008, Nadal beat Lleyton Hewitt, Novak Djokovic, and Fernando Gonzalez on the way to winning Olympic gold.

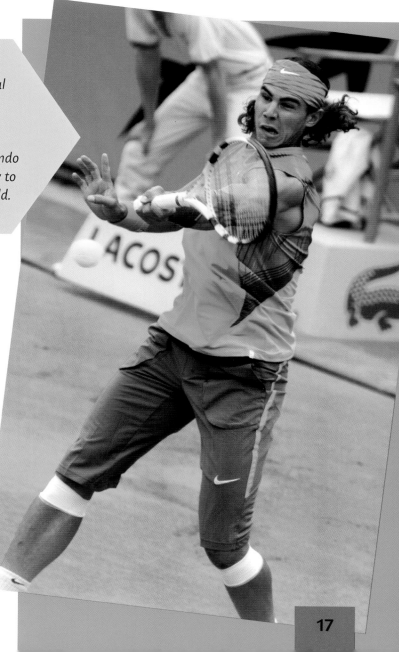

Superstar

U.S. star Andre Agassi was in fine form during the 1996 Olympics men's singles. Most finals last three to four hours, but Agassi won his final against Spain's Sergi Bruguera in just 77 minutes.

Table Tennis

Table tennis has been an Olympic sport since 1988. In many parts of Asia, table tennis stars become celebrities in the same way as basketball players in the United States or soccer players in Europe.

Wang Hao of China serves in the final of table tennis at the 2008 games. Hao and partner Wang Liqin beat the German pair, Christian Suess and Timo Boll, to win the gold medal.

TABLE TOP GAME

Players compete on a table measuring 9 ft. by 5 ft. (2.74 m x 1.525 m) divided by a net. They hit the ball across the table, making sure that the first bounce is on their opponent's side. They score a point if the ball bounces more than once on their opponent's side of the table or if one player cannot keep the ball in play.

WINNING GAMES

A game is won when a player has scored 11 points and is two points ahead of an opponent. If the score is 10–10, the game continues until they reach a score such as 12–10 or 13–11. In singles matches at the Olympics, the first player to win four games wins the match and knocks out the opponent.

BAT AND BALL

A table tennis ball is hollow and light, weighing just 1 ounce (2.7 g). Players use small rackets (also called bats or paddles) covered in rubber. Skilled players spin the ball to make it loop and swerve in the air so that it changes direction when it lands on the table. Top players also hit powerful smash shots, sending the ball flying at speeds of over 62 mph (100 km/h).

FEATS AND RECORDS

At the 2008 Olympics, Singapore won its first medal since 1960. Li Jiawei, Feng Tianwei, and Wang Yuegu won silver in the women's team table tennis competition.

FEATS AND RECORDS

China has an amazing record at Olympic table tennis. Chinese table tennis players have won 20 of the 24 gold medals awarded since 1988, as well as 13 silvers and 8 bronzes!

TEAM TABLE TENNIS

Since the 2008 Olympics, doubles table tennis has been a team competition. A country's team plays four singles and one doubles match. The first team to win three matches goes on to the next round.

China's Guo Yue hits a delicate shot against Singapore's Jiawei in the match for the women's singles bronze medal. Top players like Yue put huge amounts of spin on the ball.

Field Hockey

Field hockey is an all-action, 11-a-side team sport. Players use a wooden stick to push, flick, and hit a small, solid ball around a large field. The aim of the game is to score goals by shooting the ball past the other team's goalkeeper and into the goal.

Japan's Kaori Chiba dribbles the ball past German defenders at the 2008 Olympics. A hockey game lasts 70 minutes, split into two 35-minute halves.

Olympic OoPs

India scored a marvelous victory at the 1932 Olympic games. In front of the U.S. team's home crowd in Los Angeles, Roop Singh scored ten goals as they won 24–1. The American team next lost to Japan 9–1.

HOCKEY HISTORY

Field hockey began in the 19th century and has been played by men at the Olympics since 1908 and by women since 1980. The Olympics joins the World Cup (held since 1971 for men and 1974 for women) as the leading competition for the sport.

SQUAD AND SCORING

A field hockey team has 16 players—11 on the field and five substitutes. Players can be subbed on and off the field any number of times. The goalkeeper wears lots of protection and is allowed to handle the ball, which can travel at more than 62 mph (100 km/h). If another player touches the ball, the referee gives the ball to the other team.

Players score goals from inside a large semi-circle in front of each goal. At major tournaments, a video referee helps the on-field referee by watching replays to check whether or not a goal has been scored.

FEATS AND RECORDS
The German Keller family started its marvelous medal haul in 1936 when Erwin Keller won a silver. His son Carsten won a gold in 1972, and his grandsons Andreas (in 1992), Florian (2008), and granddaughter Natascha (2004) all won gold medals playing hockey. Outstanding!

Dutch goalkeeper Lisanne de Roever uses her stick to stop a shot during a game against China. A goalkeeper can use any part of her body to stop a shot.

Spain's Victor Sojo controls the ball while German defender Timo Wess moves to tackle him. This was the 2008 men's Olympic final, when Germany beat Spain 1–0.

GAME PLAY

Hockey players need to be fit, fast, and strong. A player uses the flat face of the wooden hockey stick to pass the ball to teammates or dribble it past opponents in a series of taps and nudges. Defenders watch and wait before tackling with the blade of their stick or poking the ball out of an opponent's control.

A hockey field is 180 ft. (55 m) wide and 300 ft. (91.4 m) long. In the past, fields at top tournaments were grass, but they are now made from artificial turf, which lasts longer.

SIMPLY THE BEST

Only the best teams play at the Olympics. Twelve women's and 12 men's teams qualify in tournaments beforehand, such as the Asian Games or the Euro Hockey competition. Teams are divided into two groups and play each team in their group. The top two from each group compete in semi-finals, then the winners play for the gold medal, and the losing sides play for bronze.

Shooting circle

Dotted line 5 yards (4.8 m) away from shooting circle

Center spot

Halfway line

25 yard (22.9 m) line

TIGHT AND TENSE

Many hockey games are close and may be decided by a single goal. In the semi-final and final of the Olympics, a game that ends in a tie goes into 15 minutes of overtime. If the scores are still tied after this, there is a penalty shoot-out, similar to the one in soccer. Each shot is taken from a penalty spot, 20 ft. (6.2 m) from the goal.

Superstar

Dutch defender Minke Booij is one of the greatest female hockey players in the world. She won a bronze medal in 2000, a silver in 2004, and, finally, gold in 2008.

FEATS AND RECORDS

The Zimbabwe women's hockey team had a last-minute invitation to the 1980 Olympics when another country dropped out. The team had just 10 days to prepare, but it went on to win Zimbabwe's first Olympic gold medal in any sport.

MEDAL MASTERS

Between 1928 and 1968, India and Pakistan's field hockey teams won gold in every Olympics. India was the all-time leader of gold medals, with eight. Recently, Germany, Australia, and the Netherlands have been the most successful countries.

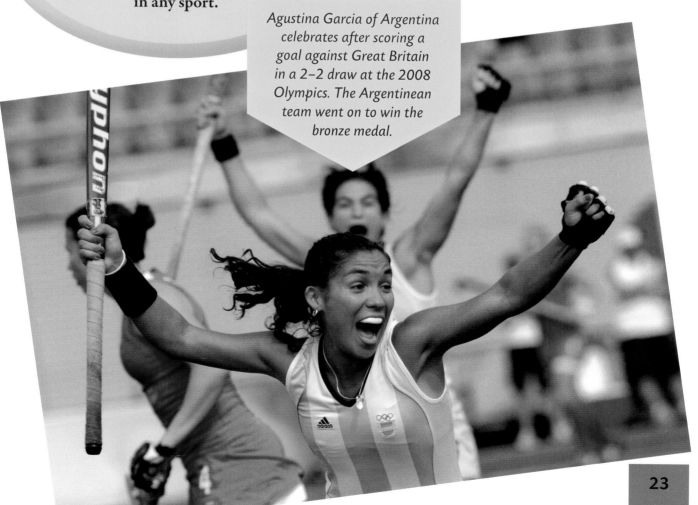

Agustina Garcia of Argentina celebrates after scoring a goal against Great Britain in a 2–2 draw at the 2008 Olympics. The Argentinean team went on to win the bronze medal.

Volleyball

Volleyball was invented in 1895 by William G. Morgan as a less energetic version of basketball. Modern volleyball is very fast, and players need to be agile and have lightning-fast reactions.

A point begins with a leaping serve made by a player from behind the back of the court into the opponent's court. A player continues serving until her team loses a point.

AIM OF THE GAME

An indoor volleyball court is 59 ft. (18 m) long and divided in half by a net that is over 6 ft. (2 m) high. Players keep a ball in the air using their hands, arms, or body. A team is allowed to touch the ball three times (with no player touching it twice in a row) before the ball must cross the net into the other team's court. Games are played in sets, with 25 points needed to win a set, but only 15 points needed to win the final fifth set.

SERVE AND DEFEND

Each point begins with a serve by a player standing behind the back line of the court. This player continues to serve until the team loses a point. Defending teams try to stop the ball from hitting the floor, diving to keep the ball in the air or leaping to block it with their arms at the net.

OLYMPIC VOLLEYBALL

Volleyball was demonstrated at the 1924 Olympics, but it did not become part of the games until 40 years later. At the 2000 Olympics, the rules were changed so that every team now has a specialty defender called a libero, who doesn't serve and wears a different colored top. Today, either team can score, regardless of who serves.

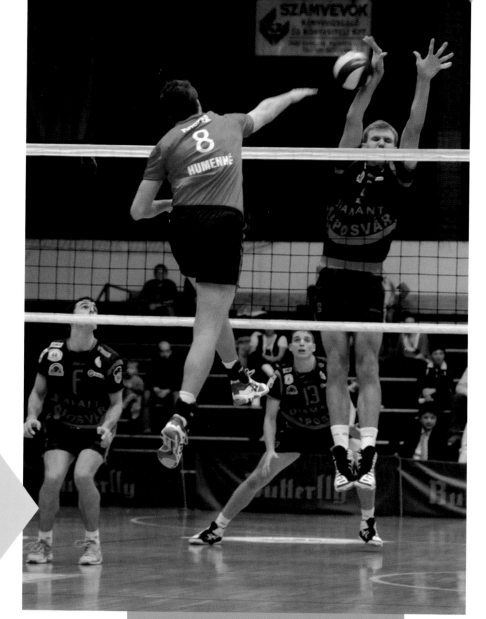

A Hungarian volleyball player spikes the ball by hitting it powerfully over the net with an overarm motion. The opposing player leaps and raises both arms to try to block the shot.

Superstar

Inna Ryskal has won more volleyball medals than anyone else. She won silver in 1964 and 1976, and gold in 1968 and 1972 as part of the Soviet Union team.

Olympic OoPs

At the 1988 Olympics, Peru's women's team was two sets up and just one point away from beating the Soviet Union, but they eventually lost the match by three sets to two.

Beach Volleyball

Beach volleyball was first played at the Olympics in 1996. It is an exciting version of volleyball with just two players per side. Both the men's and women's tournaments include 24 pairs, and every country can send two teams.

This men's 2008 beach volleyball semi-final was between two Brazilian teams. Ricardo Santos (right) has been to three Olympics, winning a silver medal in 2000, gold in 2004, and bronze in 2008.

RULES OF THE GAME

Beach volleyball has similar rules to volleyball. A team can touch the ball three times before sending it over the net. The beach volleyball ball is slightly larger and softer, and the court is covered with sand. Only two players compete, and no substitutions are allowed, so the game is a test of fitness and stamina as well as skill.

Top players are very agile and can dive sharply to retrieve a ball, as well as leaping high to block an opponent's shot at the net. Top pairs from

Superstars

Americans Misty May-Treanor and Kerri Walsh are the only beach volleyball pair to win Olympic gold medals at two Olympics in a row. When they beat China's Tian Jia and Wang Jie to win their second gold medal in 2008, it was their 108th win in a row.

A team wins a set by reaching 21 points. If the scores are tied after two sets, a third tiebreaker set is played to 15 points. Teams change sides of the court every seven points or after every five points in the tiebreaker set.

BRINGING IN THE BEACH

The beach volleyball competition at the 2012 Olympics will be held in Horse Guards Parade in the center of London. Many tons of sand will be imported into London for the arena, which will hold up to 15,000 spectators.

countries such as the U.S., Italy, China, and Brazil work closely together, and one player often sets up a teammate for a powerful overarm shot over the net called a spike. Players signal their next move to a teammate with a hand behind their back where their opponents can't see it.

FEATS AND RECORDS
Stefan Kobel and Patrick Heuscher won a bronze medal in beach volleyball at the 2004 Olympics. Not bad, considering they come from Switzerland, a mountainous country with no coast or beaches.

American Elaine Youngs dives at full stretch to try to reach the ball before it hits the sand. If the ball lands in her court, her team loses the point.

Gold Medal Greats

Many competitors train hard and make sacrifices to perform at their best at the Olympics. Competition is fierce in all ball sports, so only the most talented take part. Here are the stories of four great Olympic athletes.

VENUS WILLIAMS

American Venus Williams has been the most successful tennis competitor since the sport rejoined the Olympics in 1988. She has won three gold medals (two in 2000 and one in 2008). She has also won five Wimbledon singles tournaments and two other singles grand slam events. In the women's doubles, she plays with her sister Serena and has won a further 11 grand slam women's doubles titles, including the 2010 Australian Open.

FEATS AND RECORDS

Venus Williams recorded the fastest serve by a woman at a grand slam tournament when she hit a serve measured at 128 mph (206 km/h) at the 2007 French Open.

Venus Williams prepares to play one of her trademark powerful shots.

CHARLES KIRALY

Kiraly learned to play volleyball from his father, a Hungarian doctor, on the beaches of California. He was a member of the U.S. volleyball team that won at the 1984 Olympics and was captain when they repeated the feat in 1988. Kiraly was an athletic player with a powerful shot who also won at World Championships. He switched to beach volleyball, and with his partner Kent Steffes, he won the first Olympic beach volleyball tournament in 1996.

TEUN DE NOOIJER

Dutch field hockey player Teun de Nooijer played at his first Olympics in 1996. His skill helped the Netherlands win their first ever Olympic gold medal. The team won gold in 2000, gained a silver at the 2004 games, and finished fourth in 2008. In 2009, Teun played his 400th game for his country, winning a 5–3 victory over India.

Teun de Nooijer races away after scoring another goal for the Netherlands.

ISA LESLIE

Women's basketball star Lisa Leslie competed t four Olympics in a row from 1996, winning a old medal every time. In 2004, Leslie became he all-time leading point scorer of the U.S. vomen's team, as well as its most successful ebounder at the Olympics. Leslie captained he team at her last Olympics in 2008. She was lso the first woman to perform a slam dunk— coring by leaping above the basket and pushing he ball down through the hoop—in the WNBA rofessional basketball league.

Lisa Leslie pauses to shoot. The star basketballer scored 6,263 points during her WNBA career.

29

Glossary

agile   the abillity to move your body, or parts of it, very quickly while keeping under control

amateur   someone who plays a sport without being paid to do so

defender   a player whose main aim is to stop goals from being scored against their team

dribble   basketball players dribble by bouncing the ball with one hand while moving their feet; dribbling in soccer and hockey means moving the ball along the ground, with small taps of the feet in soccer and the stick in hockey.

formation   the way that in many ball sports a team lines up to play

forward   players whose main job is to score goals or points, or to create chances for their team to score

grand slam   the name given to the four biggest tennis tournaments— the Australian Open, the French Open, Wimbledon, and the U.S. Open

intercept   to take possession of the ball as it passes between opponents

knockout   a way of organizing a competition so a losing player or team leaves the competition and the winner progresses

mark   to guard an area of a court or field, or a player from the opposing team to prevent them from scoring

midfielder   soccer and hockey players skilled in both offense and defense who play in the middle of the field

pass   to send the ball to a teammate

penalty   a chance to score a goal in hockey and soccer with only the goalkeeper opposing you

professional   a player who is paid to play a sport as a living

rally   in tennis and volleyball, an exchange of shots between the two opposing players or teams

serve   the action that starts a point in volleyball, tennis, and table tennis, when one player hits the ball into play

stamina   the energy an athlete needs to perform hard physical exercise for long periods of time

substitutes   players who don't start a match, but come in to replace a teammate during a game

tiebreaker   a game in tennis used when the score in a set is tied 6–6; a player must be two points ahead of an opponent to win the set.

underdog   a slang term to describe a player or team not likely to win a competition

wild card an opportunity for a player to take part in a competition or tournament even though he or she has not qualified in the usual way

World Cup the leading soccer competition for national soccer teams; tournaments are held for both men's and women's soccer

Books

How to Improve at Basketball by Jim Drewett (Crabtree Pub. Co., 2008)

Modern Olympic Games by Haydn Middleton (Heinemann Library, 2008)

The Olympics: History by Moira Butterfield (Sea-to-Sea Publications, 2012)

Smash It Tennis by Paul C. Challen (Crabtree Pub. Co., 2010)

Spike It Volleyball by John Crossingham (Crabtree Pub. Co., 2008)

Web Sites

www.olympic.org/Sports
This web page lists all the sports in the Olympics. Click on a sport to find information on how it is played, Olympic champions, and much more.

www.fifa.com
FIFA runs world soccer, including the World Cup. This web site is enormous and contains videos, photos, interviews, and results from soccer all over the world.

www.nba.com
The official web site of the NBA is packed with action videos and photos of top basketball players. It has links to web pages about the WNBA and basketball all over the world.

www.allabouttabletennis.com/index.html
This web site tells you about table tennis, its best players, and the leading tournaments.

www.itftennis.com
A great starting point to learn about top tennis players and tournaments, with sections on the Olympics and the men's and women's professional circuits.

www.fivb.org
The official web site of the organization that runs volleyball around the world. It has playing guides and rules to both volleyball and beach volleyball.

Index